W9-BAH-956

The Fisherman's Tale

THE GREEN TIGER PRESS

Color separations by Colorcraft of Hong Kong.
The typeface is Signature Light, set by
Professional Typography of San Diego, California.
Printed and bound in Hong Kong.

First Edition • First Printing
ISBN 0-88138-101-2

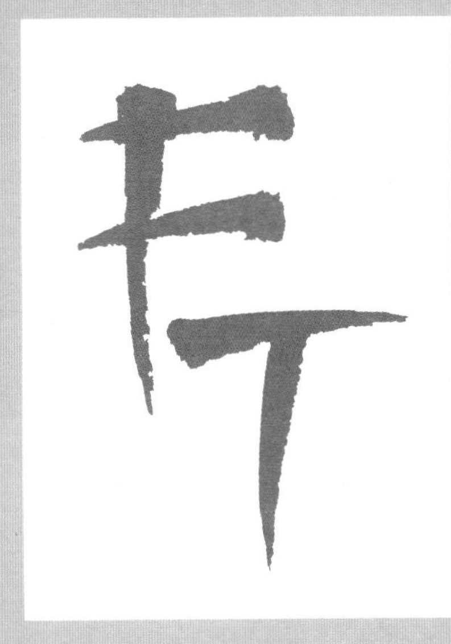

STORY BY
Emily Whittle

PICTURES BY
Jeri Burdick

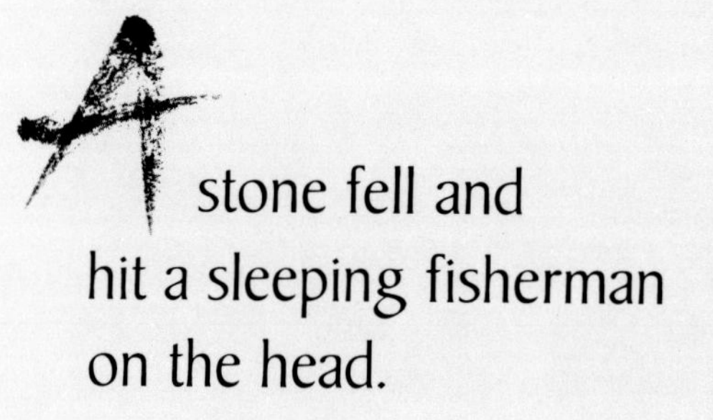

A stone fell and
hit a sleeping fisherman
on the head.

He awoke, stunned, and kicked
his fishing pole involuntarily.
The line had caught on something
and was taut!
Completely forgetting
about the lump on his head,
he struggled to reel the line in.

On the end of his line
was a large oyster.
Inside it was a lustrous pearl—
the biggest and most beautiful
he had ever seen.

He sold it for
a great price in the city
and became a rich man.

Soon, he had
forgotten how to fish.
He had forgotten how
to sing the fisherman's songs.
He became very melancholy and
went to bed with a bad headache.

While he slept,
a thief crept into his house and
stole all of his possessions,
including his new silk suit,
which had been hand-sewn
by the village tailor.

The fisherman was wakened by his stomach,
which was rumbling with hunger. When he saw
that he had been robbed, he said to himself,
"I must go to the police at once!"
But his stomach only rumbled louder.
"Well," he thought, "Perhaps first I will take
my dusty old fishing pole and try to catch
a bite of supper. Then I will have
a clear head to decide what I must do."

While he fished,
the songs he used to sing
came back to him.

The sun felt good
on his face and he realized
he hadn't been so happy
in a long time.

He caught many fish,
and went home
to a big simple meal.

Feeling full and satisfied,
he decided to take a little nap
before summoning the police.
In the golden evening light,
he nodded off, humming softly
to himself.

His peaceful dreams were abruptly
interrupted by a loud knocking at his door.
It was the police!
"Honorable Sir, we have caught a thief
wearing your fine silk suit and carrying
many expensive items," they said,
holding the scoundrel by the collar.
"We thought he must have robbed you,
since you are the only rich man in our village."
The startled man looked at them blankly.

What use have I for
fine silk suits?" he asked.
"I am a fisherman.
It is true I am a rich man,
but nothing of value has
been stolen from my house."